S0-AAA-924

JUSTICE LEAGUE UNLIMITED™

SUPERMAN™

ALLIANCE OF HEROES

written by John Sazaklis
designed by Can2 Design Group

studio fun BOOKS

White Plains, New York • Montréal, Québec • Bath, United Kingdom

On the distant planet Mars, two American astronauts, J. Allen Carter and Ed Reiss, are seeking signs of life among the red dirt and rocks. Carter and Reiss unload their high-tech equipment from the shuttle and set it up on the smoothest surface they can find among the craggy terrain.

As the machines whir to life they begin digging into the dirt. The astronauts are both hopeful and excited about what they may discover. Suddenly, their exploration is cut short by an earthquake! RRRRRUMBLE!

The ground cracks, creating a chasm beneath Carter and Reiss. Carter loses his footing and tumbles into the abyss!

The United States first launched a human into space on May 5, 1961.

CARTER, LOOK OUT!

That astronaut was Alan Shepard aboard the spacecraft Freedom 7.

2

Mariner 4 was the first spacecraft to provide up-close photographs of Mars on July 14, 1965.

The astronaut looks around the dark cavern. He sees a giant door marked with strange symbols. Carter pries it open with a pick-axe and is flooded by a blinding beam of light. Whatever horror was locked inside that chamber is now free!

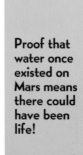

AAAAARGH!

Proof that water once existed on Mars means there could have been life!

Batman's alter ego is billionaire Bruce Wayne.

He lives in an enormous mansion named Wayne Manor in Gotham City.

When their expedition is cut short, the two shaken astronauts return to Earth. A couple of years pass and the mission to Mars is all but forgotten. It has not, however, fallen off the radar of the World's Greatest Detective–Batman!

He has been following suspicious occurrences that he feels are all interconnected somehow. So, the guardian of Gotham City treks to Metropolis on an investigation. These strange activities have one thing in common: they have been taking place at deep space research facilities across the country. Tonight, Batman makes a crack in his case!

The Dark Knight spies on three scientists. One of them displays super-strength by lifting a massive machine. He exposes a hidden piece of advanced technology. Batman deduces that the scientists are aliens in disguise and that the device could only mean one thing—trouble!

Batman is expertly skilled in martial arts as well as forensic science.

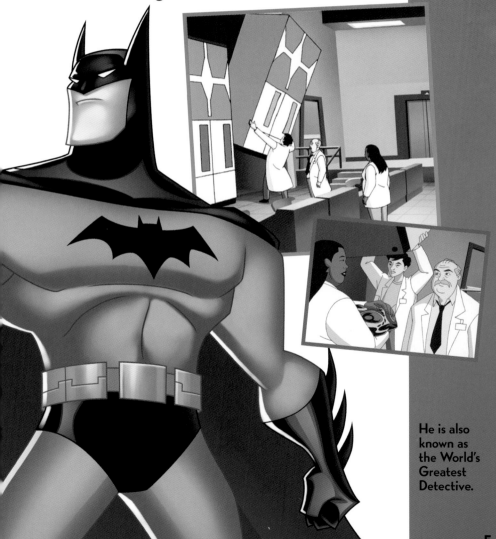

He is also known as the World's Greatest Detective.

Batman's Utility Belt contains several portable crime-fighting gadgets.

Batman follows the peculiar people up to the roof and sees them attach the device to the facility's satellite.

I DOUBT *THAT* MODIFICATION IS LEGAL.

The most popular gadget is the Batarang—a bat-shaped boomerang.

The Dark Knight springs into action, engaging the technicians in combat. He uses every gadget in his Utility Belt, but to no effect!

The alien imposters are strong and fast and ruthless! Batman is almost overpowered when a blur of red and blue suddenly appears—SUPERMAN! He is the protector of Metropolis.

Superman is really an alien from the doomed planet Krypton.

THEY DON'T LOOK SO TOUGH. NEED A HAND?

THANKS. I THINK I CAN HANDLE THIS.

His parents sent him to Earth in a tiny space shuttle when he was just a baby.

Superman's first appearance was in *Action Comics* #1, June 1938.

Superman's arrival scares away the scientists. Before the Man of Steel can capture them, he experiences a powerfully strange sensation. With his senses disrupted, Superman cannot focus. This allows the aliens to detonate their explosive device.

Superman was created by Jerry Siegel and Joe Shuster.

KA-BOOM!

Batman was created by Bob Kane.

Batman first appeared in *Detective Comics* #27, May 1939.

Batman carries his fallen friend away from the blast as the entire building collapses. All that is left is a pile of smoldering rubble. Climbing out of the wreckage eerily unscathed, the scientists head toward the forest and disappear into the night.

Superman thinks Batman is way too serious.

Superman slowly regains his balance. The dizzying effect of his alien encounter has left lingering traces of discomfort. Usually impervious to harm, Superman finds this new predicament slightly unsettling.

Batman helps the hero to his feet. Then the Dark Knight informs Superman about the security breaches that he was investigating and about how several deep space monitoring networks had been disabled. Batman is now convinced, beyond the shadow of a doubt, that the events are immediately connected to these alien creatures.

WHAT HAPPENED TO YOU?

I SAW INTENSE IMAGES, BUT NOTHING I CAN REMEMBER.

Superman is concerned, but remembers he is needed elsewhere. He hands Batman a small communicator.

Batman thinks Superman is not serious enough.

Superman's Kryptonian name is Kal-El.

Superman rushes to the World Assembly Building where Senator Carter has called a hearing. He was the astronaut that fell into the crater on the Mars expedition two years ago. Senator Carter speaks about how the freak experience changed his life.

WHEN I WAS ON MARS, I SAW HOW FRAGILE OUR PLANET REALLY IS. I PROPOSE A BOLD NEW FORCE FOR PROTECTION. A FORCE DEDICATED TO THE GOOD OF ALL MANKIND. A FORCE KNOWN AS **SUPERMAN!**

Kal-El's shuttle crashed to Earth and landed in Kansas.

The mighty hero of Metropolis enters the big, round room. Those seated in attendance are in awe of the Man of Steel. He cuts a very imposing figure but addresses the room with warmth and compassion.

Superman was adopted by farmers Jonathan and Martha Kent, who named him Clark.

I HAVE FOUGHT HARD OVER THE YEARS TO EARN YOUR TRUST. I SWEAR TO UPHOLD THE IDEALS OF TRUTH AND JUSTICE, NOT ONLY FOR AMERICA, BUT FOR THE WORLD!

Clark's super-strength and invulnerability developed at an early age, but his powers of flight emerged in high school.

S.T.A.R. Labs (Scientific and Technological Advanced Research) is located in Metropolis. It has branches in Gotham City and Paris.

Later that night, Batman breaks into an abandoned S.T.A.R. Labs building. Inside, the Dark Knight makes a chilling discovery! Mounted on the wall are three pulsing pods containing the real scientists in a state of suspended animation.

Batman wastes no time in freeing the captives. He reaches into his Utility Belt and produces a razor-sharp Batarang. Then he carefully slices through the outer shell, as gooey red slime oozes out of the pods and drips onto the ground.

Batman's work is almost finished when he hears a low rumble coming from across the room. The rumble grows into a loud growl, and a ferocious guard dog leaps from the shadows! GRROAR!

The beast lunges at the Dark Knight, baring its gleaming fangs. It claws and scrapes at Batman, who manages to swiftly escape the dog's clutches by flipping it over his shoulder into a high pile of boxes.

Suddenly, it changes shape—revealing another alien imposter! The creature overpowers Batman and hurls him through a window. SMASH! With his last bit of strength, Batman uses the signal watch to call Superman.

Superman allowed scientists at S.T.A.R. Labs to examine his Kryptonian physiology.

Superman's hearing can pick up frequencies as high as a dog whistle.

Across town, Superman's super-hearing picks up the signal watch's high frequency. *Beep-Beep-Beep!* In the blink of an eye, Superman zooms toward its location.

The Man of Steel finds Batman unconscious. He rushes to his friend and revives him. At that moment, a flaming meteor streaks across the sky! It crash-lands in a nearby public park.

Superman and Batman arrive just in time to see three mechanical appendages break out of the meteor rock. Attached to the spindly legs is a bulbous head that surveys the area with its menacing stare. Then it shoots a white-hot laser beam—incinerating everything in its path!

Superman can fly faster than a bullet. Some bullets travel as fast as 720 miles per hour!

Superman propels himself toward the malicious machine as it fires another laser beam—directly at him. The powerful blast sends the Man of Steel reeling over several city blocks!

WHATEVER THAT THING IS, I'VE GOT TO STOP IT!

Batman immediately radios his Batplane via remote control. The sleek, high-tech aircraft arrives in seconds. Batman climbs in and launches two missiles at the alien walker.

KA-POW!

Batman does not have any superpowers. His body and mind, however, are at peak levels that surpass most human development.

The explosions do not faze it one bit. But, they buy Superman enough time to make his return. The Man of Steel speeds at the monster with the force of a locomotive and punches it right into a nearby bridge.

The victory is short-lived, as two more alien walkers crawl out of the meteor. The government has deployed its armed forces into Metropolis and they arrive in tanks and fighter jets.

Metropolis is also known as the City of Tomorrow.

It is a large, wealthy city, having a population of nearly 11 million citizens.

It is referred
to as "The
Big Apricot,"
just as New
York City is
nicknamed
"The Big
Apple."

Suddenly, Superman experiences another vision. Only this time it is much more intense than what he felt at the space monitoring facility. The Man of Steel stops in his tracks and his eyes glaze over. He has entered a trance! Then, just as suddenly, he soars into the air, zooming past Batman in the Batplane.

Perplexed, the Dark Knight watches as Superman flies right out of Metropolis, becoming a tiny blue dot on the horizon!

WHERE IS
HE GOING?

In 1947 an airborne object crash-landed in Roswell, New Mexico.

Batman follows Superman to a secret government bunker. The Man of Steel is pounding on the heavy metal door with his fists.

WHAM!

HOLD IT! DESTROYING GOVERNMENT PROPERTY ISN'T YOUR STYLE. WHAT'S GOING ON?

SEE FOR YOURSELF!

Superman tears open the door and leads Batman inside. The Caped Crusader finds himself in yet another laboratory with a surprising discovery–a green man!

The U.S. Armed Forces claims it was debris from an experimental surveillance device.

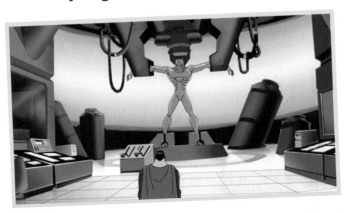

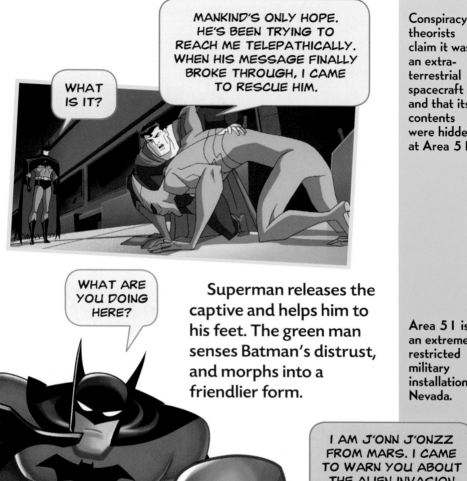

MANKIND'S ONLY HOPE.
HE'S BEEN TRYING TO
REACH ME TELEPATHICALLY.
WHEN HIS MESSAGE FINALLY
BROKE THROUGH, I CAME
TO RESCUE HIM.

WHAT
IS IT?

Conspiracy theorists claim it was an extra-terrestrial spacecraft and that its contents were hidden at Area 51.

WHAT ARE
YOU DOING
HERE?

Superman releases the captive and helps him to his feet. The green man senses Batman's distrust, and morphs into a friendlier form.

Area 51 is an extremely restricted military installation in Nevada.

I AM J'ONN J'ONZZ
FROM MARS. I CAME
TO WARN YOU ABOUT
THE ALIEN INVASION
BUT I WAS CAPTURED
AND IMPRISONED HERE.
YOUR GOVERNMENT
IS HOLDING ME FOR
OBSERVATION.

The S on Superman's chest is a Kryptonian family crest.

Superman apologizes for J'onn's mistreatment at the hands of the American government and promises to help him any way that he can.

Together with Batman, the heroes escort their new Martian friend out of the top-secret facility. Unfortunately, when they reach the exit, their path is blocked by a general and his platoon of men. The grim-looking group is armed to the teeth with heavy artillery. The general does not look happy.

Superman's suit and cape are, like him, impervious to damage.

STOP RIGHT THERE. YOU'RE TRESPASSING!

Batman adopted the symbol of the bat—a nocturnal predator—to strike fear into the hearts of criminals.

Before Superman can explain the situation, the troops transform into the angry alien invaders.

YOU'LL NEVER LEAVE HERE **ALIVE!**

J'onn J'onzz is also known as the Martian Manhunter.

The alien army attacks the heroes! One of the soldiers fires his laser cannon at the Dark Knight, but J'onn J'onzz leaps into its path and takes the hit. The Martian is wounded. Superman sees this and picks up a tank with his super-strength.

ZAP!

BATMAN, GET HIM TO SAFETY! I'LL COVER YOU!

Martian Manhunter's first appearance was in *Detective Comics* #225, November 1955.

Batman rushes J'onn to the Batplane. The aliens continue to shoot at the heroes, but Superman hurls the tank at them. SMASH! The Caped Crusader and his cargo make it to safety.

Telepathy is the ability to communicate with another using only your mind.

Once Batman loads J'onn into the aircraft, he buckles himself in and takes off. Superman follows close behind. Together, the three friends soar into the air away from their extraterrestrial enemies.

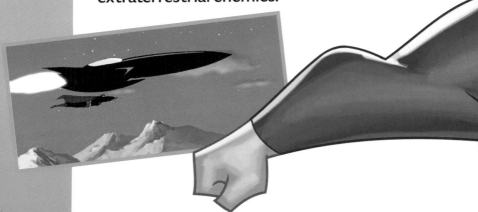

The Batplane has smart technologies like an ejector seat, autopilot, and stealth mode.

All of a sudden, a fleet of spaceships appears in the sky and fires at the Batplane. Batman expertly weaves in and out of the mountaintops, causing some of the ships to crash behind them. Superman punches through one, but several more convene around him.

The first stealth aircraft was the F-117 fighter jet. Its odd shape can reflect radar at odd angles, making it hard to track.

CRASH!

The Green Lantern Corps is an intergalactic police force based on the planet Oa.

With Superman occupied, the Batplane's wing sustains a hit and tears right off! Batman and J'onn tailspin toward the ground, spiraling in for a crash landing. Suddenly, the Batplane stops in midair. It is surrounded by a green glow.

Oa is the home and headquarters of the Guardians of the Universe.

Through the cockpit window, Batman sees the silhouette of a man wielding a power ring. He is Green Lantern–Galactic Guardian! Green Lantern safely places the Batplane in a nearby clearing.

This Green Lantern is John Stewart and he protects Space Sector 2814.

Hawkgirl is really Shayera Hol from the planet Thanagar.

Just as suddenly, one more silhouette soars overhead, wielding a powerful mace crackling with energy. It is Hawkgirl—winged warrior from Thanagar! She slams one of the spaceships into the path of another. They crash!

Thanagar's inhabitants are a race of hawkpeople.

Shayera was a lieutenant and espionage instructor for the Thanagarian military.

The heroes fight off their foes and meet in a clearing. Superman comes up with a quick battle strategy that will neutralize the immediate threat before them. Feeling the need to help, J'onn J'onzz exits the Batplane. He flies alongside Superman, Green Lantern, and Hawkgirl. The four heroes combine their forces and attack the alien aircraft with blinding speed and immense force.

Wonder Woman is really Princess Diana of the island Themyscira.

In mere moments, Superman and his amazing allies are able to minimize the terrible threat. But before the last foe falls, it blasts Hawkgirl out of the air.

As the alien aircraft closes in on her, a star-spangled hero rushes to Hawkgirl's rescue. It is Wonder Woman—warrior princess of the Amazons! She deflects the laser blasts with her unbreakable silver cuffs.

Some of Diana's attributes are speed, flight, strength, and wisdom.

PING!
PING!

Superman and Green Lantern take down the remaining ships.

The Flash's name is Wally West.

He is also a forensic scientist at the Central City Police Department.

The quiet is soon disrupted by a streaking red blur, the trademark entrance of only one hero—The Flash! The Scarlet Speedster zooms into the clearing with the Batplane's missing wing in tow.

HEY BATMAN, I THINK YOU DROPPED THIS.

Superman turns to his friends and thanks them for their help.

IT'S LUCKY THAT YOU ALL ARRIVED WHEN YOU DID.

IT WASN'T LUCK. I SUMMONED THEM TELEPATHICALLY.

WHO ARE YOU AND WHAT THE HECK IS GOING ON HERE?

MY NAME IS J'ONN J'ONZZ AND I CAME HERE FROM MARS TO WARN YOU OF AN ALIEN INVASION.

Wally's speed powers were the result of an accident in a lab where he was struck by lightning while mixing chemicals.

Mars is also known as the Red Planet.

Mars is the fourth planet from the Sun.

WE FIRST ENCOUNTERED THESE ALIEN INVADERS MANY CENTURIES AGO...

The Martian recounted his epic tale of woe. He told the heroes how these parasites invaded Mars without warning and began to systematically steal the psychic and shape-shifting abilities of its inhabitants.

The Martians armed themselves and marched into battle. They fought bravely and valiantly, but many lives were lost. The survivors devised a nerve gas to paralyze the aliens.

Donning gas masks, the Martians blasted the invaders with the toxin, immediately immobilizing them. Then they sealed the evildoers inside a large chamber so they would never hurt anyone again. This chamber was buried deep beneath the surface of Mars.

Mars is named after the Roman god of war. It has two moons, named Phobos (after the god of fear) and Deimos (after the god of terror).

Then J'onn explained how, after 500 years, the invaders were accidentally revived by an astronaut from Earth during an exploration mission. That astronaut was Senator Carter!

THIS IS JUST TOO WEIRD.

Parasites are species that live off a host body, depleting it of its energy.

With Mars depleted, the invaders had nothing left to feed upon. They came to Earth for fresh energy sources. When your government trapped me, I was powerless to stop them! The alien agents infiltrated your monitoring facilities to sneak in unobserved!

I WAS A PRISONER OF YOUR GOVERNMENT.

THAT'S WHY THEY SABOTAGED THE NETWORK, SO WE COULDN'T DETECT THEIR ACTIVITIES!

Some parasites are found in nature and can be plants like mistletoe or animals such as hookworms.

Earth is the third planet from the Sun.

Far in the distance, the heroes see a dark cloud fill the sky. It rumbles with thunder and crackles with lightning. It is a bad omen.

Meanwhile, in Metropolis, the meteor spits forth more extraterrestrial trouble. Out comes a giant machine that cracks the surface of the street and drills into the ground. Giant metallic pistons pump up and down, digging deeper into the Earth's core. The excavation causes ionized gas to fill the air.

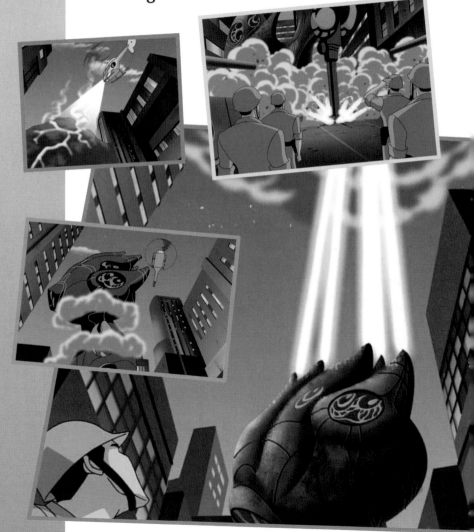

Metropolis isn't the only city under such duress. Similar events are occurring at the same time all across the globe!

WHAT ARE THEY DOING?

THE INVADERS ARE NOCTURNAL. THEY ARE USING THOSE FACTORIES TO BLOT OUT THE SUN AND LIVE IN PERPETUAL DARKNESS.

The Flash is known for his sense of humor.

Batman is not.

FRIENDS OF YOURS?

IT'S NO JOKE.

The Flash can create whirlwinds with his hands, run on water, and vibrate his molecules so fast that he can pass through solid objects.

Superman decides that the heroes must work together to defeat the invaders. To cover more ground, the Man of Steel groups them into smaller teams. Green Lantern and The Flash head out into the jungles of South America to face off against one of the factories.

Before Green Lantern can assess the situation, The Flash rushes rashly into the fray! He zooms up behind a walker and calls for its attention. When the walker turns around, it zaps a laser beam at the Scarlet Speedster. The Flash outruns the attacks and continues to taunt the machine with insults!

His disposition causes him to make hasty decisions and get into trouble.

44

The Scarlet Speedster tries to outrun the roving eye of the walker, but gets blasted by some sticky goop!

Green Lantern can create anything he imagines with his power ring—a sword, a shield, a baseball bat, even a giant fishing net.

AAAH!
I'M SORTA STUCK HERE.

SPLAT!

He can control the precision of the hard light energy beam with laser-like accuracy.

Green Lantern flies to his friend's side. He uses his power ring to slice off the robotic limb of the walker with a beam of hard light energy. Then he slices the slimy glue off of The Flash.

The Great Pyramid at Giza, Egypt, is one of the Seven Wonders of the World.

Batman, Wonder Woman, and J'onn J'onzz go to Egypt. They spy an alien factory surrounded by walkers and search for the best place to strike.

I CANNOT FIND ANY OPENINGS TO THE MACHINE.

With god-like speed, Wonder Woman uses her golden lariat to lasso a walker's legs together. She pulls tight and the creature crashes into the machine, creating a hull breach.

Wonder Woman's lariat is also known as the Golden Lasso of Truth. Whomever she ensnares with it is compelled to tell the truth.

THERE'S YOUR OPENING.

The three heroes enter the factory and meet a wave of armed guards. The aliens open fire, but Wonder Woman blocks the blasts with her bracelets. The guards see the sunlight peeking in through the hole and retreat. Batman deduces that the Sun's powerful rays may have a harmful effect on the invaders.

PING!

William Moulton Marston, the creator of Wonder Woman, also invented the blood pressure test!

47

Hawkgirl's mace is made of Nth Metal—an element with electrical and gravitational properties.

Meanwhile, Superman and Hawkgirl return to Metropolis. After wrecking one of the walkers, Superman uses its broken leg to breach the wall of the darkness-making factory. Then the heroes cautiously enter.

The atomic number of Nth Metal is 676.

KEEP A SHARP EYE OUT.

I ALWAYS DO!

Superman's
weaknesses
include
magic and
Kryptonite.

Guards rush toward the heroes. Hawkgirl
soars into action and scatters the aliens with
her magical mace.

As they head further into the core of the
machine, Superman and Hawkgirl are
sprayed with knockout gas and fall asleep.

Kryptonite is
a radioactive
element from
the planet
Krypton that
usually looks
like a glowing
green rock.

FSSSSSS!

Martian Manhunter is the sole survivor of his race and has found a new home on Earth.

Back in Egypt, Batman, Wonder Woman, and J'onn J'onzz are being pursued by alien guards. The chase leads them into a highly restricted area populated by alien drones.

LOOK! IT'S THE CENTRAL CORE.

HOW CAN WE SHUT IT DOWN?

His favorite snack is chocolate cookies.

The Martian scans the area with his enhanced vision. His attention focuses high above the chamber on an item that looks like a beating heart—it is the machine's power source!

In order to get to it, J'onn tells his friends that he will need a diversion. Batman and Wonder Woman leap into the fray, startling the alien drones. The Dark Knight and the Amazing Amazon lead the drones away from the central core so that J'onn may reach the Ion Matrix crystal unobserved.

The human heart is about the size of a fist and beats about 100,000 times a day!

THE ION MATRIX CRYSTAL! IF WE CAN REMOVE THAT WE'LL SHUT DOWN THE WHOLE PLANT.

Wonder Woman bridges the gap between man's world and Themyscira as an ambassador for peace and justice.

J'onn J'onzz flies to the matrix and disconnects it from the machine's main hub. He gets blasted by a drone and drops the crystal. Wonder Woman rushes to the rescue, picks up J'onn, and then flies them both out of the machine.

Batman will do anything for his crime-fighting cause, even sacrifice himself.

Before Batman makes his escape, he runs back to grab the Ion Matrix. The drones place the area on lockdown and all the exits are blocked—trapping the Dark Knight inside!

At that very moment, scientists at Mission Control discover a much larger flying object headed toward Earth. They confirm that it is another alien spaceship—five times bigger than the landers that have already invaded!

A mission control center manages aerospace flights from liftoff to landing.

MY READINGS ARE OFF THE CHART!

NASA's mission control is the Kennedy Space Center located on Merritt Island, Florida.

John Stewart, AKA Green Lantern, is also an architect and a former Marine.

Leaving Batman behind, Wonder Woman and J'onn J'onzz head to Metropolis where the city is in grave danger. Green Lantern and The Flash arrive moments later.

Standing atop a skyscraper, the four heroes see a darkness-making factory pumping away in the distance.

The Flash is known as the Fastest Man Alive.

SUPERMAN AND HAWKGIRL ARE TRAPPED IN THERE.

The Imperium first entered the solar system roughly 1,000 years ago.

The heroes approach the factory, but soon discover that it is guarded by one of the walkers.

Thinking quickly, The Flash streaks toward the sentinel and throws a rock at its head.

TAG! YOU'RE IT!

Always in a rush, The Flash wears a spring-loaded ring which releases his costume instantly!

The walker rapidly fires its laser beams at The Flash, but the Scarlet Speedster is faster. He escapes each blast without breaking a sweat!

IS THAT THE BEST YOU GOT? *FBBBT!*

The Flash zigs and zags and zooms, confusing the sentinel and causing it to trip over itself. The walker crashes to the ground and erupts in an explosion of flames.

BUH-BYE!

The only thing faster than The Flash's feet is his mouth!

BOOM!

Martian Manhunter can mind-link with his teammates, allowing each member to communicate telepathically with one another.

Once inside the factory, J'onn uses his psychic abilities to track down Superman and Hawkgirl. He senses their presence on the other side of the main chamber. Green Lantern creates a hard-light laser cutter with his power ring and carves a hole through the wall. Superman and Hawkgirl are inside—hanging upside down!

GREAT HERA!

Before the heroes can complete their mission, the wall seals up and locks them inside. Then they are sprayed with the same toxic gas that took down their friends!

Bats, not hawks, are creatures that usually sleep upside down!

IT'S A *TRAP!*

At that very moment, an enormous spaceship enters the Earth's atmosphere. It descends rapidly. Shrouded in a dark cloud, the spaceship hovers right over Metropolis. Thunder rumbles and lightning streaks across the sky.

Stricken with fear, the remaining citizens of the city scream and flee for their lives.

Atmospheric entry occurs at a little over 62 miles from the Earth's surface.

Soon after the effects of the knockout gas wear off, the heroes revive and find themselves bound to the floor. They pull and strain, but the bonds are impossible to break. One of the aliens approaches them and transforms into a familiar face.

If this Senator Carter is really an alien imposter... then the real Carter must still be on Mars!

SENATOR CARTER!

At that moment, the bay door opens and the enormous mother ship enters the loading dock. Imperium disembarks and floats toward his subjects. Bowing to their leader, the aliens chant in unison.

A squid is a marine animal characterized by its large head and long arms or tentacles.

The rotund, squid-like creature flails its appendages in appreciation. It surveys the prisoners and stops when it recognizes an old foe.

J'ONN J'ONZZ! FINALLY, I WILL FINISH WHAT WE STARTED LONG AGO.

Imperium ensnares the Martian with his tentacles and begins to sap his energy, reverting J'onn to his original form. The other heroes are unable to help their friend.

Squids contain an ink sac that can expel a cloud of dark liquid into the water as a form of camouflage—much like the Imperium invaders.

NEVER!

ZZZARK!

Not only is Batman a skilled martial artist and detective, he is also a brilliant inventor.

Suddenly, a dark figure swoops into the chamber. It is Batman! The Dark Knight escaped from the factory just in time to rescue his friends. He slices through the matrix core with a razor-sharp Batarang.

Batman inserts an ingenious gadget that reverses the polarization of the Ion Matrix Crystal. Now, instead of a cloud of darkness, the factory will pump a beam of light into the sky!

In mere moments, the thick thunderclouds begin to dissipate. Warm rays of sunshine brighten the chamber. The alien invaders scatter in fear and run for cover. Those not fast enough disintegrate in the sunlight.

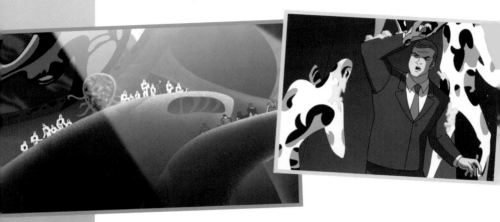

Superman's Kryptonian physiology is enhanced by the Earth's yellow Sun, giving him his amazing abilities.

With one mission accomplished, Batman begins his second—freeing his friends. He explains his discovery.

COMING FROM THE DEPTHS OF SPACE, THESE ALIENS HAVE NO RESISTANCE TO THE SUN'S RADIATION.

This gives the weakened J'onn J'onzz a bright idea. Struggling with all his might, the Martian grabs a hold of Imperium's tentacles and drags him into the light. The alien conqueror's skin begins to bubble and burn. He slowly releases his hold on J'onn.

Bats are nocturnal animals. They are awake at night and sleep during the day.

AAARGH!!

EW! THAT'S ONE NASTY SUNBURN!

Writing in pain, Imperium calls his subjects to his side and screams a command.

The aliens, including the Carter imposter, fire their laser cannons at the heroes.

The Justice League's first appearance was in *The Brave and the Bold* #28, February/ March 1960.

Their first foe was a giant alien starfish named Starro the Conqueror.

With his powers recharged by the Sun, Superman breaks free of his bonds in an instant. He flies up into the air, enjoying the wind as it rushes past him. It is time to level the playing field.

With his super-strength, the Man of Steel rips up a chunk of the ground and curves it upward as a makeshift shield. Superman protects his friends from the alien laser beams while he uses his heat vision to blast them free. ZAP!

Like starfish, Martian Manhunter has the ability to regenerate his body parts.

The Green
Lantern
Oath is: "In
brightest day,
in blackest
night, no evil
shall escape
my sight.
Let those
who worship
evil's might,
beware my
power—
Green
Lantern's
light!"

Green Lantern rockets into the air and
cracks his knuckles. The Galactic Guardian
has been itching to use his power ring and the
aliens are the perfect targets. He encases
them in an escape-proof force field.

IT'S TIME TO
FIGHT WITH
LIGHT!

Hawkgirl stretches her wings and soars high into the air. Then she swoops down and smashes into another group of aliens with her mace.

Hawkgirl and The Flash have a special friendship. He thinks of her as an older sister, only shorter.

WHAM!
BAM!
CRASH!

The invaders call for reinforcements. As they march into the chamber, The Flash zooms past and knocks them off their feet. He delivers a flurry of punches and kicks so rapid that the aliens do not know what hit them!

Superman's amazing abilities include flight, super-speed, invulnerability, heat vision, X-ray vision, super-hearing, super-strength, and freeze breath!

To help defeat the invaders, Superman punches a hole in the roof of the factory. More sunlight streams in! Weaving in and out, the Man of Steel keeps punching holes as if he were threading a needle.

To become Wonder Woman, Amazons competed in a grueling competition of strength and skill. Princess Diana was the winner.

Wonder Woman and Green Lantern follow Superman's lead. The Amazing Amazon tears it apart with her bare hands while Green Lantern blasts through with his power ring.

Imperium panics at the increased amount of sunlight. He needs to escape but J'onn J'onzz holds him in a vise-like grip. The alien conqueror zaps the Martian with an electric current and breaks free!

Martian Manhunter is thought by some to be as strong as Superman.

71

The word doppelganger means "double goer" in German.

It was first used in English literature in the year 1851 to describe the physical double of a living person.

As Imperium retreats into the mother ship, the Senator Carter imposter runs after him. In a desperate attempt to flee, the doppelganger latches on to Imperium's tentacle.

UNHAND ME, WORM!

TAKE ME WITH YOU, MASTER!

Imperium slaps the imposter away and he lands directly in a ray of light. The alien sizzles and melts away into a puddle of goop.

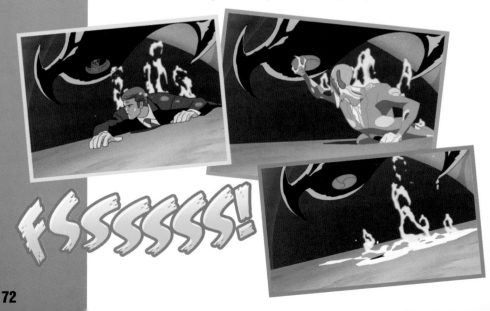

FSSSSSS!

Wonder Woman notices Imperium and his mother ship taking off into the sky. She flies up and lassoes the tail end of the ship with her golden lariat.

Wonder Woman was the first female member of the Justice League.

Hawkgirl rushes to aid her Amazonian ally by smashing the mother ship with her mace. The magical weapon causes the ship's exterior to crack and crumble. The vessel veers out of control and collides with the machine.

As the structure collapses, Superman discovers a hidden chamber filled with pods. Slumbering within are innocent humans! He calls out to his friend for help.

FLASH, GIVE ME A HAND!

Humans spend about a third of their lives sleeping. That's about 25 years of shut-eye!

The Man of Steel uses his heat vision to cut open the sleep sacs. The Flash is there to gently catch the prisoners. After they are all freed, Green Lantern swoops by and picks the group up in a protective bubble.

EVERYBODY STAY CLOSE. THIS PLACE IS GOING TO BLOW!

The others pair up and make their way to safety. Wonder Woman flies with Batman in tow, while Superman carries The Flash as the cloud-making factory erupts.

Superman's intense heat vision can be adjusted to blast an area as wide as a football field or as microscopic as a speck of dust.

Earth is the densest planet in our solar system.

With barely a second to spare, everyone reaches a clearing as the machine explodes. Imperium's mother ship is annihilated in the blast.

KA-BOOM!

It measures 24,901 miles all the way around!

Unlike most other planets, Earth has only one moon.

The super heroes watch as the remaining thunderclouds disappear and sunlight bathes the ravaged city of Metropolis.

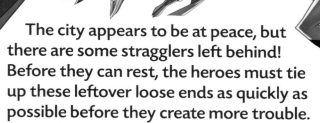

The city appears to be at peace, but there are some stragglers left behind! Before they can rest, the heroes must tie up these leftover loose ends as quickly as possible before they create more trouble.

Working together with expert precision and impeccable teamwork, Superman, Batman, Wonder Woman, The Flash, Green Lantern, Hawkgirl, and J'onn, destroy the remaining invaders in no time. Earth is safe once again!

On a nearby television screen, an army general voices his concerns.

The first Americans to land on the Moon were Neil Armstrong and Buzz Aldrin on July 20, 1969. The name of their spacecraft was Apollo 11.

WE GOT LUCKY THIS TIME. WHAT WILL WE DO IF THE INVADERS EVER RETURN?

Bruce Wayne is the owner of many research and development companies, including WayneTech.

This gives Superman an idea. He builds an outer space watchtower that orbits the Earth. This watchtower has state-of-the-art security systems, surveillance equipment, training areas, dormitories, and a hangar for all sorts of vehicles.

He helps fund the Justice League's outer space watchtower.

THIS WILL ACT AS AN EARLY WARNING SYSTEM FOR DETECTING OTHER THREATS FROM SPACE. IT WILL BE OUR BASE OF OPERATIONS.

AND IT HAS A FULLY STOCKED KITCHEN!

Superman invites the other heroes to the watchtower so that he can explain its purpose.

Batman has an underground headquarters called the Batcave.

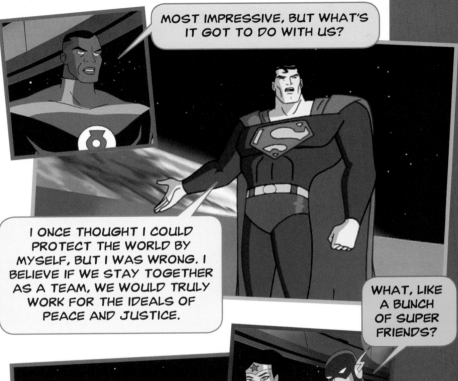

MOST IMPRESSIVE, BUT WHAT'S IT GOT TO DO WITH US?

I ONCE THOUGHT I COULD PROTECT THE WORLD BY MYSELF, BUT I WAS WRONG. I BELIEVE IF WE STAY TOGETHER AS A TEAM, WE WOULD TRULY WORK FOR THE IDEALS OF PEACE AND JUSTICE.

WHAT, LIKE A BUNCH OF SUPER FRIENDS?

MORE LIKE A *JUSTICE LEAGUE!*

Superman's secret hideaway is the Fortress of Solitude. Located in the Arctic, it is where he keeps remnants of his home world.

To access the outer space headquarters, the super heroes travel via teleporters called "slideways."

The heroes are keen on Superman's idea and want to be a part of his new super hero team. They vow to serve and protect planet Earth. With their forces combined, no challenge is too great for the Justice League!

Since its inception, the Justice League has had over 60 members!